Ivy
and
the
Goblins

Also by Katherine Coville

Ivy

The Cottage in the Woods

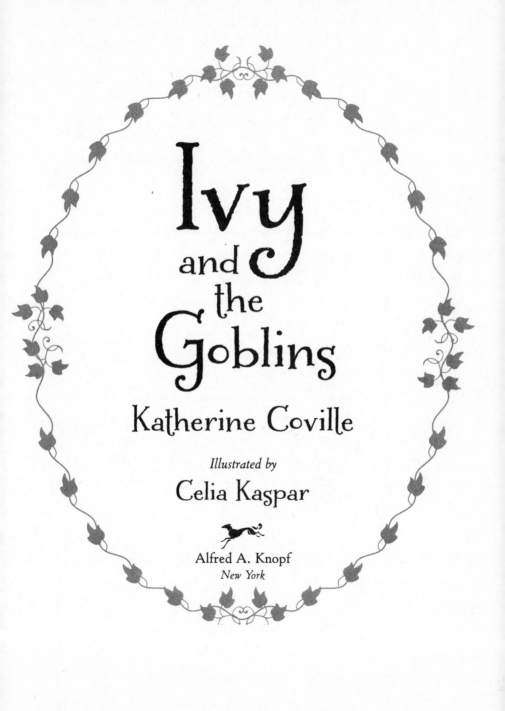

Ivy
and
the
Goblins

Katherine Coville

Illustrated by

Celia Kaspar

Alfred A. Knopf
New York

Visit us on the Web! rhcbooks.com

Educators and librarians, for a variety of teaching tools, visit us at RHTeachersLibrarians.com

Library of Congress Cataloging-in-Publication Data
Names: Coville, Katherine, author. | Kaspar, Celia, illustrator.
Title: Ivy and the goblins / Katherine Coville ; illustrated by Celia Kaspar.
Description: First edition. | New York : Alfred A. Knopf, 2019. | Summary: After a farmer brings them a goblin egg, Ivy and Grandmother are stuck with a shrieking, mischievous baby until Ivy decides to brave the dark forest to find the goblin's family.
Identifiers: LCCN 2018026939 (print) | LCCN 2018033570 (ebook) | ISBN 978-0-553-53981-3 (ebook) | ISBN 978-0-553-53979-0 (hardback) | ISBN 978-0-553-53980-6 (glb)
Subjects: | CYAC: Goblins—Fiction. | Animals—Infancy—Fiction. | Animals, Mythical—Fiction. | Human-animal relationships—Fiction. | Healers—Fiction. | Grandmothers—Fiction. | Orphans—Fiction. | BISAC: JUVENILE FICTION / Fantasy & Magic. | JUVENILE FICTION / Animals / General. | JUVENILE FICTION / Family / General (see also headings under Social Issues).
Classification: LCC PZ7.1.C6845 (ebook) | LCC PZ7.1.C6845 Ix 2019 (print) | DDC [Fic]—dc23

The text of this book is set in 17-point Cloister.

Printed in the United States of America
March 2019
10 9 8 7 6 5 4 3 2 1

First Edition

For Melanie
—K.C.

Contents

CHAPTER 1

Happily Ever After

Once upon a time, there was a small, round girl named Ivy, who was doing her best to live happily ever after. Ivy lived with her grandmother, Meg the Healer, and that made her happy. Ivy had Grandmother's big, overgrown garden to play in, and that made her happy. Ivy even had her own work to do every day, and that made her happy too.

Her work was helping Grandmother take care of sick and injured creatures. Some of them were forest animals, like rabbits, raccoons, or foxes. Some of them were magical creatures, who had come to be her friends. One was a three-legged griffin. Another was an aging dragon. And a big hive of friendly pixies lived in a hole in the oak tree, and followed Ivy everywhere! Ivy loved all the creatures, and they loved her, and so they let her feed them and tend to them, and that made Ivy very happy indeed.

Grandmother's garden was a wonderful place. It was right on the edge of the tidy village of Broomsweep, next to the Dark Forest, in the small kingdom of Evermore. Grandmother's cozy cottage sat right in the middle of the big, overgrown garden. The garden was brimming with flowers and shrubs and weeds of all colors and kinds. It was full of good things for Grandmother to use in her potions. And it was the perfect place for Ivy and her friends to play hide-and-seek. It had comfortable holes and dens of different sizes, hidden here and there, that sick animals might inhabit while Ivy and Grandmother took care of them. And sometimes, even after a creature was all better, it liked living in the garden so much it would move right in and stay there.

That was how they met Cedric, the three-legged griffin. He was a big, beautiful griffin, with a front part like an eagle and a back part like a lion, but he had lost one back leg in an accident. Cedric had come to the cottage one night, asking for help. He needed to learn how to land on just three legs without crashing, and he needed a place to live. So Grandmother and Ivy had welcomed him. They helped him learn to make graceful landings. They became such good friends that the griffin stayed on, in an enormous nest behind the cottage.

Each morning, when Ivy went cheerfully about her work, Cedric greeted her from his big nest in the back of Grandmother's garden.

"Good, good, good morning! Very good! Most good!" he would say, in his strong eagle voice, as he wagged his lion tail.

"Good morning, Cedric!" Ivy would reply. Then a tiny white dog would pop out from under Cedric's wing and yap happily. His name was Poof. He had big brown eyes and a little pink tongue. Even though he was very small, he was not at all afraid of the griffin. He liked to live with Cedric and hide under the griffin's huge wings. As soon as breakfast was finished, the griffin would make a mighty leap and fly to the top of the cottage roof, so he could keep watch over all of Grandmother's garden.

"I guard the garden!" he would say. "Griffins guard!"

"Good Cedric!" Ivy would say.

"Yes, good Cedric," he would answer. "Mighty Cedric!"

Then Ivy would sprinkle seeds on the ground, near the hazel trees, for the birds and squirrels.

She visited every creature in the garden to see if they needed food or fresh bedding. One morning, she took care of a rabbit with an infected ear. Then she comforted a porcupine who was missing some of her quills. Then she tended to a small mole with a toothache. She always petted the creatures who needed petting. She was extra careful when she petted the porcupine. She spoke softly to the animals, just like Grandmother did. Even though they didn't understand her, they seemed to like the sound of her voice.

If Grandmother asked her, Ivy even gave them some of the special tonics Grandmother cooked up. She might give them Sneezlewort Potion, for sneezes, or Limberjuice, for aches and pains. She was always very sure to measure carefully and do everything the way Grandmother told her. She wanted to be a healer, just like Grandmother.

When Ivy made her way about the garden, the pixies flitted all around her. They were tiny winged people, smaller than Ivy's pinky finger. Sometimes, they had tiny temper tantrums. When someone made them mad, the pixies might poke or pinch them, or pull their hair. But when they were happy, they tickled Ivy's neck and laughed tiny laughs like wind chimes. They did somersaults and twirls and all sorts of tricks in midair. They rode on her head and shoulders while she went about her work, and made everything more fun. Ivy was delighted to have them for friends. Every day, she put a cup of honey in the hole in the oak tree, where the pixies lived. The pixies loved honey. And they loved Ivy. She felt like the luckiest girl in the world.

When Ivy had finished with her chores, she would go down by the stream and visit Balthazar, the dragon who lived under the weeping willow tree. He was small for a dragon, but even so, Ivy had been a little apprehensive around him when he first came to the cottage, looking for a cure for a dreadful fiery sneeze. (It can be a terrible thing when a fire-breathing dragon sneezes!) But when she got to know him, Ivy found that Balthazar was very old and wise, and had many stories to tell. After a few doses of Grandmother's Sneezlewort Potion, he had stopped sneezing fire. He stayed under the weeping willow tree, where he was usually napping.

Sometimes, Ivy's human friends came to the garden to visit as well. Peter, who lived next door, used to tease her, until she had showed

him how to make friends with the pixies. Now he was nice to Ivy, and they often laughed together as he helped her care for the creatures. Edwina and Marta, the shoemaker's daughters, had come to be good friends with Ivy and Peter too, and sometimes joined them to play games in the garden.

All in all, it was a great place for living happily ever after. And Ivy did. Until, one day, something happened.

CHAPTER 2

The Noise

It didn't seem like trouble at first. It started out as an ordinary day. Farmer Higley brought his sick goat to Grandmother. Grandmother listened while he explained that the goat seemed to have a stomachache. Grandmother called Ivy to come and help. Ivy held the little goat's head and spoke soothingly to him to keep him calm, while Grandmother looked him over.

Grandmother gently felt his swollen belly. She opened his mouth and peeked down his throat.

"Hmm," she considered. "I think he has eaten something he shouldn't have. A very common problem with goats!"

"Well," said Farmer Higley, "one of my old boots is missing. Could he have eaten that?"

"You never can tell with a goat," Grandmother answered. "Ivy, please fetch the Bellyache Tonic, the special kind for curious goats. Measure one small cup, and mix it with a handful of oats."

Ivy went into the cottage and opened the potion cupboard. She began to read the labels: "Whisker Oil . . . Rash-Be-Gone Rub . . . Sore-Ear Cure . . . Bellyache Tonic . . . Here it is! Special Bellyache Tonic for Curious Goats!" Ivy picked it up and checked the label again. She used a small cup to measure the liquid, and scooped a handful of oats from a big open bag. After mixing them carefully in a wooden bowl, she took the oats out to feed to the goat. The goat sniffed at them, then he chomped them right up. Then he tried to eat the bowl! Ivy laughed and took it away.

"That should do it," Grandmother said to Farmer Higley. "If he's not all better by tomorrow, bring him back."

Farmer Higley smiled and thanked her. That was when the something happened. He said, "As payment, I have something special that I found in the forest. I was walking in the Dark Forest and got a little lost. While I was trying to find my way, I saw this hidden in a fern bed. I don't know what it is. I've never seen anything like it before. I thought you might want it." He lifted a wooden crate out of his cart. It was filled with straw, and on the straw sat one big egg.

Ivy stared at the egg, her eyes wide. The egg was almost as big as the cantaloupes growing in the garden. It was orange, and covered with dark brown speckles. What could be in there? She looked at Grandmother's face, but Grandmother did not look happy.

"Oh dear," Grandmother said. "I don't know what it is either, but I think you should have left it alone. Can you put it back where you found it?"

Farmer Higley's face fell. "I'm afraid I could never find the same place again. Does that mean it won't hatch?"

"I don't know," Grandmother answered, shaking her head. "If you can't put it back, I guess we'll just have to take care of it and see what happens." With that, Grandmother thanked him and said goodbye. Ivy followed her inside, burning with curiosity, as Grandmother placed the crate in a warm spot next to the fireplace. Then they stood back and contemplated the egg.

"What kind of egg *is it,* Grandmother?" asked Ivy.

Just then, Ivy heard a scratching sound coming from the egg.

"Quickly," replied Grandmother, "we should look through my books and see if we can find something like it. My old eyes are not so good. Read the titles for me, dear."

Ivy went to the bookshelves and started looking. First she pulled up a stool to stand on, and tried the top shelf. "Let's see. . . . *Fine Feathered Friends.* This one is about birds, Grandmother. Wouldn't it tell about their eggs?"

"I'm afraid this is much too big to be a bird's egg," Grandmother answered uneasily. The scratching noise from the crate grew louder.

"How about a lizard egg or a snake egg?" Ivy asked.

Grandmother shook her head. "Lizard and snake eggs are too small. You'd better look for something about magical creatures. I only hope—"

"What, Grandmother?"

A cracking sound came from the egg.

"Never mind. Just keep looking. Hurry."

Ivy stepped down from the stool and looked all through the next shelf, and the next, but she found nothing about magical creatures. Finally, she looked along the bottom shelf. Some of those books were very old and very dusty. The last book on the bottom shelf was *The Beastly Book of Magical Creatures and Monsters*. Ivy pulled it out and blew the dust off it, then she set it on the table in front of Grandmother. There were more cracking sounds from the egg.

Grandmother opened the book and looked at the pictures. "I just hope it's not—"

"What, Grandmother?"

Grandmother didn't answer. Ivy stood next to her and turned the pages, reading each page out loud.

"Basilisk?" she read.

"No . . . ," Grandmother said.

"Cyclops?"

"No . . ."

"Dryads? . . . Dwarves? . . . Elves?"

"No . . . no . . . no."

"But look at this picture, Grandmother! *'Melon-sized eggs,'* it says. *'Orange, with brown speckles.'* That's the one, all right." She looked over at the egg as the cracking sound continued. She watched as a little chip of the egg fell away, and suddenly a terrible, whiny, screeching sound came out of the egg. The terrible noise increased with each piece of eggshell falling away. Grandmother and Ivy looked on anxiously, their eyes wide.

CHAPTER 3

Born Hungry

Just then, the egg opened right up, and out tumbled a wrinkled, little creature with grayish skin. It had a big, round, bald head, with pointed ears, big, round eyes, a button nose, and tiny, blunt fangs. Its mouth was wide open, like a hungry baby bird's.

"That's just what I was afraid of," Grandmother said, raising her voice in order to be heard.

Ivy looked closer at the book and read the

words below the picture. Her eyes grew even wider. "It's . . . a *goblin*!"

Ivy turned to Grandmother. "What do we do now?" she asked.

"I don't know. I've never seen a baby goblin before," Grandmother admitted. "See what it says in the book."

Ivy read from the section on goblins. "It says that they're born hungry. It says they eat mushrooms, but they must never eat— Grandmother, part of the page has been torn away."

"Oh dear. How will we ever know what they *mustn't* eat?"

The baby goblin wobbled slowly onto his oversized feet, and reached his chubby, little arms up to Ivy, as if he wanted to be picked up. Ivy thought he was cute, in an ugly sort of way. "Aww," she said, reaching out to him. As soon as she touched him, he bit her hand.

"*Ouch!*" she hollered, pulling her hand away and shaking it. "I guess he really *is* hungry!"

"Be careful," Grandmother said. "He may look harmless, but—"

The baby goblin stared at Ivy with his big dark eyes, and stopped yowling for a second. Then he started right up again.

"Why does he have to be so *loud,* Grandmother? Do all babies screech like this? How can we make him stop?"

"We'll just have to take care of him the best we can. We'd better hurry and find something for him to eat. He should be safe here in the crate," Grandmother said. "He's too little to climb out. You look for mushrooms on the north side of the garden, and I'll try the south."

Grandmother and Ivy grabbed some baskets and headed for the door. The baby goblin screamed even louder to see them go.

Ivy hurried through the garden to a damp, shady patch where she had seen edible mushrooms growing. She could still hear the little goblin making his big noise inside the cottage as she began to pick.

"What is that racket?" a deep voice thundered. Ivy looked around. Balthazar, the dragon, had come up the path from the stream. His nostrils were blowing smoke. "The sound woke me up from my morning nap!" he said.

Cedric, who was sitting on top of the house, guarding the garden, called out: "What, what, what is that terrible noise? Awful noise! Squalling noise! It hurts Cedric's ears!"

Ivy turned back to them. "It's a *baby*," she said. "A baby goblin. It just hatched."

"Oh . . . ," Cedric answered. "How terribly awful! How do we get rid of it?"

"Grandmother says we must take *care* of him, Cedric. I have to pick some mushrooms for him."

"Will that keep him quiet?" asked the dragon. "I'll help you look!"

"Thank you, Balthazar. That would be a great help!"

The dragon went about the garden, sniffing here and there, and pointing out some likely spots to Ivy. They found brown mushrooms and red ones and some with spotted caps. Grandmother had taught her which kinds of mushrooms were safe to eat. Ivy knew the red and spotted ones were not good to eat. She picked only certain special mushrooms that she knew were safe. Soon Balthazar called out that he had found some more, and Ivy hurried to pick them. Then she thanked Balthazar for his help and rushed back to the cottage, where she met Grandmother.

When they opened the door, a terrible sight met them. Grandmother had been wrong. The baby goblin had climbed out of the crate and up the table leg, onto the tabletop. Half of Grandmother's pots and jars had been knocked over, their contents spilled. The baby had found the bag of oats and dumped them all over everything. He was sitting in the middle of the mess, still squalling, throwing oats up in the air.

"Oh no!" cried Ivy, dropping her basket.

"Oh dear," groaned Grandmother. "He's learned to climb already!"

The baby goblin struggled to his feet and held his arms up to Ivy, to be picked up. Ivy didn't want to get bitten again, so she decided to try feeding him first. She plucked some mushrooms out of her basket and popped one in his mouth. The baby stopped his shrieking and gobbled the mushroom right down. Ivy kept feeding him— two more, then three more, then four—until he didn't seem to want any more. His tummy was nice and round.

"Go to the cupboard and get some old cloths," said Grandmother. "We'll use them for diapers." Ivy did as Grandmother said, and then watched as Grandmother showed her how to tie them around the baby's bottom.

"Now maybe he'll go to sleep," Grandmother said. She picked up the baby and put him over

her shoulder, patting him on the back, until—
BUUURRRP!—he burped a giant burp. Ivy gig-
gled as she wondered how such a big burp could
come out of such a small creature. Then Grandmother laid him back down in the crate full of
straw. Ivy watched as the baby goblin closed his
eyes and drifted off to sleep. Ivy breathed a big
sigh of relief. "Finally!" she whispered.

Without waiting to be asked, Ivy got out the
broom and started sweeping the floor, while
Grandmother picked up her potion-making pots
and bottles. She washed them out and put them
away in the cupboard, then she began to clean
up the spilled oats and potions from the tabletop.
Before they could finish clearing the mess, there
came a knock at the front door. With that, the
baby woke up and started his terrible screeching
again. Ivy peeked out the window and saw that
it was Mistress Peevish, the mayor's wife, in her
fancy purple dress. Ivy groaned. Now the day

was getting even worse! It seemed like Mistress Peevish was always angry about something. Reluctantly, Ivy opened the door.

"Good morning, Mistress Peevish," Ivy greeted her politely. "How are you today?"

Mistress Peevish had a frown on her face. "Never mind that," came the reply. "I'm here for my little dog, Foof. I know you've got her here somewhere. I've been looking all over for her!"

"I haven't seen her either," Ivy answered. She knew Foof often came to the garden to visit Poof, but she thought that sometimes Foof just came to hide. Even Ivy wanted to hide when Mistress Peevish came calling.

"And what's that terrible racket?" Mistress Peevish snapped. "I can hardly hear myself think!"

"It's the baby," said Ivy as Grandmother picked him up and bounced him gently.

"Why don't you help Mistress Peevish look

for Foof?" Grandmother called to Ivy. "I'll take care of this one."

"This one WHAT?" yelled Mistress Peevish. "That baby doesn't look like anything I've ever seen before! And why is it making so much *noise?*"

"*He's* a baby goblin," Grandmother answered. "He just hatched."

CHAPTER 4

Something in the Shadows

"A GOBLIN!" Mistress Peevish cried. "You can't have a *goblin* here! They're vicious! What will become of us?"

"He's only a baby!" Grandmother said.

"But it's a GOBLIN! You must get rid of it at once—before it turns on you and throttles us all in our beds!"

"But he's only a baby," Grandmother said

soothingly. "Besides, goblins don't throttle people in their beds."

"How do YOU know?"

"Well, at least, I don't *think* they do," said Grandmother.

"Heaven only knows what kind of damage it can do!" Mistress Peevish shouted, shaking her finger in Grandmother's face. "And listen to that noise! It can't be allowed!"

"He's a *baby*," said Grandmother, once again. "He'll quiet down in a while. We need to be patient."

Suddenly Ivy heard someone calling at the back door. When she opened it, Cedric stuck his head in and squawked, "It's started again! *Aawk!* How can we live with that awful, terrible, dreadful noise?"

Ivy had to holler to make herself heard. "Grandmother says he'll quiet down in a while. We'll just have to be patient."

Grandmother shushed the baby and bounced him, rocking her body back and forth. Soon he went from screeching to just whimpering. Mistress Peevish stood at the front door, with her hands on her hips, while Cedric stared in from the back door. Both of them looked angry.

"Griffins don't like goblins!" Cedric cried, backing away from the doorway.

"People don't like goblins either!" Mistress Peevish added. "Now, what are you going to do about it?" she asked Grandmother. "You can't keep it here!"

"I don't know *what* to do about it," Grandmother said, "except take care of him." The baby was quiet now, and she laid him back down in the box of straw. "Besides, you know our town welcomes magical creatures. Goblins are magical creatures too."

"I'm sure we never meant to welcome *goblins* into our town! I'm telling the mayor about this. He'll certainly have something to say about it! This can't be allowed! Now help me find my dog, and be quick about it! I have to get home for my tea party."

"Ivy, dear, would you help Mistress Peevish look for Foof?" Grandmother asked her. Ivy really didn't want to, but since Grandmother asked her, she agreed. She and Mistress Peevish went into the garden, calling Foof's name along the way, but Ivy didn't see a sign of the little golden-furred dog.

They followed several pathways through the garden, calling and calling, but Foof didn't appear. Cedric had retreated to his nest, with his wings covering his ears. Ivy went to him and shouted out loudly, "It's okay, Cedric. The baby is quiet now."

Cedric folded his wings back and sighed. "Too, too, too terrible," he moaned. Poof was in Cedric's nest too. Ivy called him, and he jumped out of the nest and came to her. Poof was a free dog, who didn't belong to anyone, but he liked to live with his friend Cedric, and he loved Ivy.

"Maybe if we follow him, he'll lead us to Foof," Ivy suggested.

"Where's Foof, boy? Go find Foof!" Ivy said, secretly giving him the hand signal to sit. Poof looked at Ivy, then sat down. "Find Foof!" Ivy said again, giving him the signal to stay. Poof didn't budge. Ivy was glad. She patted Poof's head and whispered, "Good boy!"

"I'm afraid Foof doesn't seem to be here today," Ivy said to the mayor's wife, smiling inwardly. She thought Foof was afraid of Mistress Peevish's temper, and that Mistress Peevish held the little dog too tightly.

"You!" cried the mayor's wife to Cedric. "You have eagle eyes! Look around and find my dog!"

Cedric stared back at her, the feathers on his forehead standing up.

"It's all right, Cedric," Ivy reassured him.

Cedric cocked his head to one side, considering. Then he turned slowly all the way around in his nest, until he was looking back at them again. "No," he said. "Not a sign of her. But there *is* something hiding under the hazel trees."

"There is?" Ivy said. "What is it, Cedric? Can you see?"

"Cedric can't see through the leaves, but something is making them rustle. Bigger than a dog. Smaller than a troll. Maybe a cow."

Ivy looked toward the hazel trees. She could see dappled shadows beneath them, but she couldn't make out any shape there. She decided to go closer and began to make her way quietly through the garden. Mistress Peevish followed her. Ivy turned and whispered, "Shhh! Whatever it is, we don't want to scare it."

As they drew nearer, Ivy caught a glimpse of something moving in the shadows under the hazel trees. It did seem bigger than a dog and smaller than a troll, but she didn't think it was a cow. She thought she heard sniffling. Finally Ivy saw something move again, and the something . . . was shaped like a horse and spotted all over. Its spots blended in with the surroundings, making it hard to see.

"Hello?" called Ivy.

There was a rustling and more sniffling.

"Hello?" called Ivy again.

"Oh. H-h-hello," came the answer. "Don't mind me. I'm just standing here."

"Have you come to see my grandmother, the healer, about something?" Ivy asked.

"Well . . . yes," the voice quavered, "but she probably can't help me. I'm afraid no one can help me." There was another loud sniffle.

"My grandmother can solve all sorts of problems," said Ivy. "Or maybe I can help. You can tell me."

Mistress Peevish looked on with her hands on her hips. "Why don't you hurry up and tell her? She's supposed to be looking for my dog! Have you seen a little, golden-furred dog?"

"N-no. I'm sorry. I haven't," said the voice from the shadows. "I wasn't paying any attention. I've been too unhappy."

"But why?" asked Ivy.

The creature slowly stepped out of the shadows and into the sun. Now Ivy could see that it looked like a horse dappled with black spots. The spots were all different sizes and shapes. And she saw something else—the horse had a horn, like a unicorn. But she had never heard of a unicorn with spots. "Ohh!" she said. "What are you?"

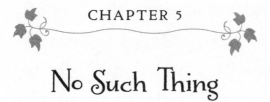

CHAPTER 5

No Such Thing

The spotted creature hung its head and sniffled again. "That's just it," the creature said. "What am I? I wish I were a unicorn, but who ever heard of a unicorn with spots? Can you help me get rid of these spots?"

"Well, you can't be a real unicorn, that's for sure," put in Mistress Peevish. "There's a unicorn pictured on the tapestry that hangs on my wall at home. It's beautiful—with a shining, spotless coat and a long, flowing mane—and you don't look anything like it!"

"See?" said the beast.

"Maybe it's a disease!" said Mistress Peevish, backing away. "Maybe it's catching!"

Ivy tried to think of what Grandmother would say.

"What is your name?" Ivy asked the creature.

"My name? My name is Branwen."

Ivy thought harder. What would Grandmother ask?

"Branwen, have you always been spotted like this, or did the spots just appear?"

The creature sniffled again. "I've been like this as long as I can remember. Ever since I was a little filly. My mother and father are real unicorns. They didn't know what to make of my spots. No one does."

"Well, maybe you're one of a kind!" Ivy cried. "A spotted unicorn!"

Branwen looked surprised, then she sniffled one more time, as if she were considering.

"A spotted unicorn? But there's no such thing!"

"There is *now*, and you're it!"

Branwen's eyes widened. "But I don't want to be it! I want to be like the others. Oh, woe is me. Only one spotted unicorn, and—wouldn't you know—I'm it!"

Mistress Peevish hung back. "I still think it might be a disease," she warned. "If you're smart, you'll keep your distance!"

Ivy reached her hand up and stroked Branwen's soft muzzle. "I don't think so at all," she murmured. "I think my grandmother would like to meet you, Branwen."

"Just don't say I didn't warn you," Mistress Peevish put in spitefully. "And you're supposed to be looking for my dog, remember?"

"Yes, Mistress Peevish," Ivy replied politely. "I remember."

"Well, I have to go home, but *you* keep looking! Bring her to me if you find her. And tell your grandmother to get rid of that goblin!" commanded Mistress Peevish. As she went away, she called, "Foof! Here, Foof!"

Ivy watched her go and sighed.

She pretended to look around for the little dog as Mistress Peevish left. Then she decided she was done.

She turned to Branwen. "Please come out. You don't need to hide anymore," Ivy said to her. "I think you're perfectly beautiful! Would you like to meet Grandmother?"

"Can she take away my spots?"

"I don't know. We'll have to ask her. Come on!"

As Ivy and Branwen headed back toward the cottage, Ivy saw a flash of golden-colored fur under the azalea bush. *Foof!* Ivy smiled and looked the other way.

Then Cedric called out from his nest, "Who, who, who goes there?"

"This is Branwen, the spotted unicorn," Ivy called back. "She's here to see Grandmother."

"Friend or foe?" Cedric demanded.

"Friend!" declared Branwen and Ivy at the same time.

"Pleased to meet you," Cedric responded cheerfully. "Ever so pleased."

As they spoke, Ivy heard a buzzing sound around her head. She looked up and saw a cloud of tiny pixies flitting all about them. They were landing on Branwen's forelock and mane. "Pixies!" Ivy cried. "They're welcoming you, Branwen. They must like spotted unicorns!"

"They *like* spotted unicorns?" Branwen asked, sounding puzzled.

"Of course!" Ivy replied. She opened the back door of the cottage and called for her grandmother. Grandmother came to the door. "Look who has come to see us!" Ivy said.

Grandmother's eyes lit up as she saw Branwen. "My, how unusual!" she exclaimed. "A spotted unicorn. I've never seen such a thing. How magnificent!"

"See?" cried Ivy. She introduced Branwen to Grandmother, and explained that Branwen wanted her spots removed.

"But you're so beautiful just the way you are," said Grandmother.

"But I'm not like a real unicorn," Branwen complained. "Ask anybody. Besides, real unicorns can heal the sick and wounded with their horns. My horn doesn't work. Please, can't you remove these spots?"

"If I could remove your spots, you'd look just like any other unicorn."

"That's exactly what I want," Branwen said.

"Oh, that's too bad," Grandmother said. She thought for a moment, then said, "I do have some spot remover, for stains on clothes, but I've never tried it on a creature before. And I don't have much of it. Maybe we could try it on one spot and see what it does? If that's what you really want."

Now Branwen's eyes lit up. "Oh yes! Please. Let's do it!"

Just then, there was a shriek from the crate with the baby goblin in it. Then another shriek. And another. Branwen backed up, with a neigh of surprise, and the pixies scattered and flew away.

"What is that noise?" Branwen cried.

"That's the baby goblin," Ivy answered. "Maybe he's hungry again."

"I suppose we had better feed him first, just in case," Grandmother responded. "I'm sorry, Branwen, but we'll have to try the spot remover later, after we've taken care of the baby."

"All right. I guess I can wait," Branwen replied.

"I do hope that noise stops soon," wailed Cedric as he hopped out of his nest and fluttered back up to the rooftop. "Griffins don't like screechy goblin noises."

CHAPTER 6

Trouble

Once again, Ivy and Grandmother took care of the hungry goblin baby, who snatched up the mushrooms like he was starving. He gulped and drooled, and snapped at Ivy's fingers, and when he was full, he let out another mighty *BUUURRRP!* Grandmother changed his diaper, then he wanted to play. Grandmother let him climb up the table again, and gave him a big spoon to bang on the tabletop. That kept him happy for a while, but soon he wanted to play something else. The baby goblin leaped off the tabletop onto a bag of dried beans and laughed. The bag split open, and beans scattered all over the floor.

Ivy got out the broom and started sweeping. Then she grabbed the baby just as he climbed to the top of the table again. He was about to leap off onto a bag of alfalfa. "No you don't!" said Ivy. The little goblin squirmed and squiggled in her hands. Then he began to scream, so she set him down on the floor. Ivy said to Grandmother, "Shouldn't we give him a name?"

"I looked it up in the book of magical creatures," Grandmother replied. "The book says goblins generally name themselves after things in nature, like kinds of weeds or rocks."

"So maybe we could call him Hemlock? Or Toadflax? Or Flint?"

"I like them all," Grandmother commented. "You pick."

Ivy watched the baby as he climbed back up the table leg. Then he leaped off the tabletop onto the bag of alfalfa and clung to it. Fortunately, the bag didn't burst. Ivy thought about burdocks, the thistle-like weeds in Grandmother's garden that stuck in her skirt and stockings. "How about Burdock," she asked, "because he clings to things?"

"That will do nicely," Grandmother said. And so it was decided.

After Burdock had finally fallen back to sleep again, Grandmother brought her jar of spot remover out to Branwen. "Which spot would you like to try this on?" she asked. "Mind you, I don't know what it might do."

"I'll take that chance," Branwen answered. "Pick any spot!"

"All right," Grandmother said. She put some spot remover on a cloth. Then she rubbed the cloth all over a small black spot on Branwen's hind leg. Branwen turned her head to watch. Grandmother and Ivy watched too. At first, nothing happened. Then the spot turned bright orange. They all watched in alarm as the spot slowly faded . . . into a funny mustard color! They looked on, waiting for it to change, but it stayed that way.

"Oh dear," Grandmother said. "I didn't mean for that to happen! Shall I try a little more?"

"Yes, maybe that will do it," said Branwen.

Grandmother rubbed more spot remover on the yellow spot, and they all watched breathlessly to see what would happen. They waited . . . and worried. The spot stayed mustard yellow. Now Branwen was a black-and-white unicorn with one yellow spot on her leg.

"Well, it doesn't show too much," offered Ivy, trying to make the unicorn feel better.

"Maybe it will fade away overnight," said Branwen hopefully.

"I'm sorry," said Grandmother. "I guess this formula needs some work. Maybe a touch of chickweed or sassafras."

"Yes," Branwen agreed. "Why don't we have a second try with a different formula?"

"If you're sure you really want to," Grandmother said doubtfully. Before she could say another word, there was a yowl from within the cottage.

"Every time we turn around, he's hungry all over again!" Ivy said with dismay.

"Isn't it good that he has us to take care of him?" Grandmother said. "Come and help me with him. Branwen, you are welcome to make yourself at home in the garden. I'll see if I can come up with a better formula, and we'll give it another try tomorrow."

When Ivy and Grandmother went inside, the baby was already climbing out of his crate. Ivy grabbed the basket of mushrooms, and Grandmother grabbed the diapers. "Here we go again!" sighed Ivy.

All that day, the baby kept Ivy and Grandmother busy. When he wasn't hungry or sleepy, he was climbing the chairs or the table or the cupboards. Ivy and Grandmother chased him and fed him and tried to get him to take naps. By nighttime, Ivy was completely tired out. She tried to soothe Baby Burdock, bouncing him gently on her shoulder, while Grandmother made a new spot-removing potion for Branwen.

"Grandmother," she asked, "how long does it take for babies to grow up?"

Grandmother set aside the potion she was making and took Burdock from Ivy's shoulder. "I'm not sure," Grandmother said. "But most magical creatures grow up quickly. We'll just have to keep on doing our best until he can take care of himself."

When Burdock fell asleep, Grandmother laid him down gently in the crate, and Ivy covered him with a blanket. Ivy finally got to eat her supper, and afterward, she was so tired she dropped into her own bed with all her clothes on.

It seemed like Ivy had barely begun to sleep when the squalling woke her up again. It was dark in the cottage, except for the glow of a single candle, and Grandmother was in her nightgown, tending to Baby Burdock.

"Isn't he even going to sleep at *night*?" moaned Ivy.

"Probably not until he's older," Grandmother replied drowsily. "Just get some rest. I'll take care of him."

Ivy turned over and was trying to ignore the baby's cries when she heard a knock on the back door. Grandmother was busy with the baby, so Ivy dragged herself out of bed and opened the door. There was Cedric, looking miserable. His eyes were only half open, and his feathers were all rumpled.

"This noisy noise," he groaned, "it's keeping Cedric awake! Too bad. Too, too bad!"

"Oh, Cedric," Grandmother called, "I'm sorry the baby woke you up."

Then Poof came to the door and started yapping. Foof was right behind him, and she was yapping too. The baby's screeching got louder. Then Ivy heard Balthazar's voice coming from the garden.

"How cad a dragon get ady sleep?" he cried. "I'b so tired! Ad I thik I feel a code cobing on!"

Soon there was a pounding on the front door too. Ivy answered the door, only to find their neighbors Jacob the Baker and his wife, Bertha, on the front step in their nightclothes. They looked *very* unhappy. "What is all this uproar?" Jacob demanded. "How are we supposed to sleep at night with such caterwauling going on?"

"I'm so sorry," replied Grandmother. "It's the baby. He'll quiet down when we feed him."

"What kind of baby makes a noise like that? It's terrible!" said Bertha.

"Well, actually," Grandmother answered, "it's a goblin baby."

"A GOBLIN!" cried Jacob and his wife together. "No wonder!"

"You can't have a goblin here," exclaimed Jacob. "You'll have to get rid of it!"

"Make it be quiet!" called Cedric from the back door.

"Bake it go away!" hollered Balthazar from the garden.

Poof and Foof yapped and yapped.

Ivy didn't know what to do.

CHAPTER 7

Balthazar's Advice

Grandmother looked around at everyone. "Go back to bed. All of you!" she said. "We are just going to have to put up with some noise for a while. Now let me take care of this baby!"

At this, the neighbors made grumpy faces, but they turned and went home. Balthazar went back to his willow tree. Cedric went back to his nest. Poof followed Cedric, and Foof followed

Poof. Ivy took some mushrooms out of a basket and helped Grandmother feed Burdock until he stopped his noise and finally went back to sleep. By then Ivy was so exhausted she could hardly keep her eyes open. She and Grandmother went back to their beds and were soon asleep too.

Morning came too early. Ivy and Grandmother were awakened by the squalling baby goblin as the sun came up, and the routine started all over again. Ivy saw that Burdock seemed to have grown already. She wondered how long it would take for the baby to learn to take care of himself. When Burdock was fed and burped and his diaper was changed, Ivy had her own breakfast of oatmeal and raisins. Then she went out to take care of the other creatures in the garden. Grandmother told her which potions to give to each one.

As Ivy passed Cedric's nest, he did not perk up and say, "Good, good, good morning!" to her the way he usually did. Instead he stuck his head under one wing and moaned, "Not enough sleep!" Even Poof and Foof seemed too tired to bark.

Ivy said, "Good morning," anyway and went about her work.

Soon her friend Peter came and joined her. "That goblin baby sure makes a lot of noise," he said. "My whole family couldn't sleep last night!"

"I know," Ivy replied. "Me neither. How about helping me out?"

"All right," Peter responded. "Where do we start?"

"I'll show you. I have a surprise for you!"

Ivy took Peter to meet Branwen under the hazel trees and introduced them to each other. "Wow," Peter exclaimed. "I've never seen a spotted unicorn before! In fact, I've never seen a unicorn at all!"

"I'm not a real unicorn," Branwen sighed. "Can't you tell? Besides, real unicorns can heal sickness with their horns. My horn never worked."

"Oh," said Peter. "That's too bad. I like your spots, though."

"Would you like some oats for breakfast?" Ivy asked.

"Thank you," said Branwen. "But I couldn't sleep last night, and I've lost my appetite."

Next, Ivy and Peter visited the rabbit with the ear infection. They fed him and stroked his silky fur, and Ivy gave him some of Grandmother's Sore-Ear Cure. They could hear the baby goblin begin to squawk in the cottage. The rabbit laid his ears down flat on his back, as if it hurt to listen.

When they were done with the rabbit, they went on to see the porcupine who had lost some of her quills. Ivy gave her Grandmother's Gro-Quill Potion. She petted her—very carefully—and told her that she was still a very lovely porcupine. Then they heard Baby Burdock scream some more, and the porcupine made all her quills stand up and quiver.

Ivy meant to give a tiny pinch of Grandmother's Never-Fail Toothache Powder to the mole with the toothache. But the mole wouldn't come out of hiding.

Worst of all, when she went to place a cup of honey in the hole in the oak tree, where the pixies stayed, she found the hole was empty. Where were the pixies? Ivy and Peter looked and looked for a long time. They looked all around the garden. They called and called for them, but there were no pixies anywhere. At last, the children went inside. Grandmother was chasing Burdock while he ran squealing about the cottage. "The pixies are gone!" cried Ivy.

"Oh dear!" Grandmother said. "Are you sure?"

"We've looked in their hole in the oak tree and all over the garden. We've called and called, but they don't come. I think they've gone away."

"Perhaps the baby's noise has driven them off. I believe pixies are quite sensitive to loud noises," said Grandmother.

Ivy's shoulders drooped. "I miss them. They always make me laugh."

Peter said, "Me too."

"Yes, we'll miss them," said Grandmother. "Perhaps they'll come back when things are quieter."

Ivy sighed heavily. First there was the constant noise, then the messes, then the sleepless night. Now even her beloved *pixies* were gone! Ivy couldn't take it anymore. "Burdock is spoiling *everything*!" she cried.

"There, now," Grandmother said sweetly. "He's only a baby. He can't help himself. Besides, a good healer takes care of everyone, even goblins. Now, why don't you take a basket out and gather some more mushrooms? We're going to need them."

"All right," Ivy said, picking up a basket, "but it won't be the same without the pixies around."

Ivy and Peter went out into the garden. Ivy

wondered where to look for more mushrooms. She decided to see if Balthazar would help her find them, as he had before. They made their way to the stream, where the dragon usually napped under the weeping willow tree. When they found him, he was snoring. Wisps of smoke drifted out of his nostrils.

"Oh, Balthazar," Ivy called. "Won't you please wake up? I could use your help!" She remembered to say "please," because Grandmother had always taught her to be very polite to dragons.

Balthazar snorted, then opened one eye. Before he could answer her, Burdock shrieked so loudly that they heard him all the way from the cottage. "Dot agaid!" Balthazar groaned, with his stuffy nose. "I just got back to sleep!"

"I'm sorry," Ivy said. "Grandmother is trying to keep him quiet. We just don't know very much about caring for baby goblins!"

"Where did he cobe frob?" Balthazar asked. "Baybe you could put hib back."

"Farmer Higley found the egg in the Dark Forest. We can't put him back there! What would become of him?"

"Well, then, baybe you could find his parents. They bust be subwhere in the Dark Forest too!"

Ivy shivered. She had always been a little afraid of the Dark Forest.

"But the forest is huge," objected Peter. "It goes on for miles! How could you find his parents in such a big place?"

"Hmm," the dragon said thoughtfully. "Baybe

you could search frob the air. I ab just too sick and too tired to be buch help. But baybe Cedric could take you flyig over the forest to look for goblins."

"That's a great idea!" said Peter.

"I don't know," said Ivy. "I'll have to talk to Grandmother about it. But right now we need help finding more mushrooms to feed the baby. Could you sniff some out for us, like you did before?"

"I'b afraid by dose is too stuffed up to do ady sdiffig," Balthazar said, "but I'll cobe ad help you look."

An Accident

Later, after Peter had gone home, Ivy returned to Grandmother and the baby with a basket full of mushrooms. Ivy tried to ignore the noise, like Grandmother was doing. It wasn't easy.

"Grandmother," Ivy called, raising her voice to be heard. "Balthazar thinks we should find Burdock's parents. Do you think we can? Balthazar is sick, but Cedric could fly me over the Dark Forest so I could look for them."

Grandmother considered this for a moment. "I'm afraid it would be very dangerous to go looking for goblins!" she exclaimed. "What would you do if you found some?"

"I don't know. Ask them if they're missing an egg?"

"I know very little about goblins, but I believe they are quite unfriendly. Perhaps we'd better read more about them in that *Beastly Book of Magical Creatures and Monsters*. Look it up for me, dear."

Ivy got the book from the lower shelf and opened it on the table. She turned the pages until she reached the picture of the goblin's egg. She read the section out loud.

" '*Goblins: Magical creatures of great ugliness, full of evil or mischief. The three main types are cave goblins, forest goblins, and mountain goblins.*' "

Grandmother nodded. "Farmer Higley said

he found the egg in the forest, so read the part about forest goblins."

"Let's see. . . . 'Forest goblins: *Found in the deepest, darkest areas of forestland and sometimes swamps. They are the least friendly of the three goblin types. They live in huts made of mud and sticks, and generally eat mushrooms, tree bark, and some small animals. There are rumors that they also eat people, but there is no hard evidence to support this. Do not approach forest goblins in their natural habitat, as they will protect their territory violently. In fact, given how dangerous they are, do not approach them at all!'* "

"That settles it!" said Grandmother. "You simply mustn't go searching for any goblins! We'll have to solve the problem some other way."

Just then, there was a big crash. Ivy jumped, and turned to see that Burdock had climbed the cupboard and knocked off Grandmother's dishes. The dishes lay broken in pieces on the floor.

"Oh dear!" sighed Grandmother. "What will he do next?" She reached for the broom while Ivy held the wiggly little goblin tightly in her arms. Quicker than you can say "Oops!" Grandmother's foot slipped on one of the pieces of the broken dishes. She fell down on the floor with a *boom!*

"Oh, OW!" Grandmother cried.

Ivy put the baby in the crate and hurried to her side. "Grandmother!" she cried. "Are you all right?"

"I've twisted my ankle!" Grandmother exclaimed.

Ivy's heart was thumping. "Here, put your arm around my shoulder, and I'll help you up!"

Ivy put her arm under Grandmother's arm and tried to help her up. Grandmother huffed and puffed and groaned, but finally she was able to stand up on one foot.

"Help me to my bed," said Grandmother, and so Ivy did. Grandmother sat on her bed, in the corner of the room, her leg propped up on a pillow. She took off her shoe and stocking, and looked at her ankle. It was swollen. "Oh dear," she said. "I'm afraid it's sprained. I'll have to stay off it for a while!"

By then Burdock was already climbing out of his crate, yelping as loudly as ever. "Bring him over to me," said Grandmother. "I can hold him on my lap while you sweep up the mess. Be careful!"

Grandmother held the squirming, squalling baby while Ivy very carefully swept up the broken dishes. All she could think about was Grandmother's sprained ankle. This was too much! How could they keep this baby goblin when he caused such trouble? Ivy looked at the squirming baby as Grandmother tried to hold him still. Suddenly she felt sorry for him.

"Poor baby," she said. "You don't belong in a cottage, do you? Grandmother, how are we going to manage now? I can't do it all by myself!"

"You always do a very good job taking care of things," Grandmother assured her. "I can still help a little with Burdock. As for the rest, just do your best. That will be good enough."

But would it? Ivy didn't know.

"Bring me that basket of mushrooms, and I'll feed him," said Grandmother, holding him tightly on her lap. Ivy fetched the basket. Soon Burdock was chomping down his lunch.

Ivy finished cleaning up the broken dishes. When the baby was done eating, she tried to change his diaper. She did her best, but he wiggled and squirmed, and the diaper didn't stay up too well. Burdock took off to climb the tabletop, with his diaper sagging down around his bottom.

Just then, Ivy heard a knock on the front door.

CHAPTER 9

Mistress Peevish

When Ivy answered the door, there stood Mistress Peevish in her fancy purple dress, her face red with anger, as usual. Next to her stood the mayor, biting his fingernails.

"The mayor has come to tell you that you can't have a goblin here! *Didn't you?*" demanded Mistress Peevish, poking her husband in the ribs.

The Honorable Dudley Peevish let out a little

squeak and said, "Yes, my dear. That's right."
Then he went back to chewing on his fingernails.

"But what else can we do with the baby?" Ivy
asked. "Where can he go?" Just then, Burdock
made a run for the door. Ivy caught him in time,
but he shrieked louder than ever.

"You'll have to figure that out yourselves!"
exclaimed Mistress Peevish. "And where is my
dog, Foof?" she added. "She still hasn't come
home. I'm terribly worried about her!"

Grandmother called out from her bed in the
corner, "Come in, Mistress Peevish. Come in,
Mayor. Let's talk this over."

"My grandmother hurt her ankle," Ivy explained. "She can't get up."

"So who is taking care of things here?" demanded Mistress Peevish, entering the cottage.

Ivy looked around and said, "I am."

"What nonsense! A mere *child* taking care of
this whole place? You'll never be able to do it!

Will she?" said Mistress Peevish, poking the mayor in the ribs again.

Ivy thought about all the things she needed to do now, and she wondered if Mistress Peevish was right. But didn't she *want* to take care of things the way Grandmother did? Maybe she just needed some help. Then she got an idea.

"Mistress Peevish, I do need some help. Would you make some willow bark tea for my Grandmother? She needs it to ease the pain in her ankle."

Grandmother smiled at Ivy, then looked at Mistress Peevish. "That's just exactly what I need. Perhaps you would be good enough to help out?"

Mistress Peevish looked as if she couldn't believe her ears. "Me? Help you . . . ? Why, the *idea* . . . !" Then, as she looked at Grandmother's swollen ankle, her expression softened a bit. It got a *little* less red. She even seemed a *little* sorry for

Grandmother. "Well," she said, "I guess I could make a pot of tea—but *that's all*!"

Ivy smiled. "I'll get the willow bark," she said. She placed Burdock in his crate and got a small bag of shredded willow bark from the cupboard. Then she brought in more firewood from the woodpile so Mistress Peevish could make the cooking fire nice and hot. By that time, Burdock had climbed out of his crate and was banging his favorite spoon on the floor.

While Mistress Peevish poured water into the teakettle and hung it above the fire, Grandmother called out, "Measure four small spoonfuls of bark into the teakettle, and let it steep in hot water until it cools off. Then pour it all through a cloth to take the bark out."

"I know how to make tea!" Mistress Peevish returned. "You don't have to tell me!" She stood with her arms folded and watched Burdock playing and hollering while they waited for the water to boil. The mayor stood behind his wife, chewing on his fingernails, and didn't say a word. Finally Mistress Peevish cried, "That baby's diaper is sagging! It's going to fall off! Doesn't anybody here know how to properly put a baby's diaper on?"

"I guess I didn't do it quite right," confessed Ivy. "Will you show me how?"

"Oh, for heaven's sake!" cried Mistress Peevish. "Bring me a fresh diaper and hold him down!"

Ivy did as she said, and Mistress Peevish changed Burdock's diaper, tying the fresh diaper around him firmly. "See?" she said. "Like that!"

Just then, Grandmother looked at Ivy in a certain way, so she remembered to say, "Thank you, Mistress Peevish."

"Never mind!" Mistress Peevish replied. "It doesn't change a thing. You've got to get rid of this goblin! *Don't they?*" she said to the mayor, poking him in the ribs yet again.

"Oh yes! Yes, my dear!" Mayor Peevish responded as Burdock started to squeal even louder. "They certainly do!"

Finally the water boiled, and Mistress Peevish took the teakettle off the fire and poured the hot water into a pot of willow bark. "Now we'll go look for my little Foof while this cools off!" she said.

"But what will I do with the baby while we're outside? Grandmother can't chase him," objected Ivy.

Mistress Peevish picked Burdock up and thrust him into her husband's arms. "Here!" she said. "Make yourself useful! *You* can look after him."

"But . . . but . . . but," spluttered the mayor as Burdock screamed in his ear.

"But nothing! And see that he doesn't go near that pot of hot tea!" said Mistress Peevish. She took Ivy by the arm and stalked out the cottage door.

CHAPTER 10

Confidence

Ivy and Mistress Peevish went outside and looked all over the garden, calling for Foof. Poof stood in front of Cedric's enormous nest, as if he were guarding it, but Foof was nowhere in sight.

"Pardon me," said Branwen when they came to look under the hazel trees. "But when will the new spot-removing potion be ready?"

"It's ready now," Ivy replied, "but Grandmother

has hurt her ankle and can't get out of bed. Maybe I could try it for you. Right now we're looking for Foof, but I'll come back again later."

Ivy led Mistress Peevish down the path to the stream to see Balthazar. He was trying to nap. He lay under the weeping willow tree with one eye open, moaning softly.

"Balthazar, are you awake?" Ivy asked. Mistress Peevish stayed behind her, feeling not quite safe so near a dragon, even a smallish one.

"I'b dot asleep, if that's what you bean. Who could sleep with all this doise?" the dragon complained. "By code is gettig worse!"

"I'm sorry the baby has been keeping you up. At least the noise is not as bad down here. I've come because we're looking for Foof. Have you seen her?" Ivy asked, hoping that he had not.

"I haven't seed her id quite a while. If she has ady sedse, she's far away frob here!" declared the dragon.

"Yes, you're probably right," answered Ivy,

making sure Mistress Peevish heard her. "She's probably far away from here!"

Mistress Peevish insisted that they continue to search the garden anyway, so they went on looking and calling for Foof for a long time, but she never appeared. Finally, they returned to the cottage to see if the tea had cooled off. Burdock was shrieking louder than ever as he ran about the room, with the Honorable Mayor Peevish running after him. The mayor had lost his hat, and sweat ran down his brow as he gasped for breath. Ivy grabbed the little goblin as he whisked past and held him in her arms while Mistress Peevish poured the tea through a cloth, and filled a mug for Grandmother.

"Thank you most kindly," Grandmother said, and she took a long sip. "This is the tastiest willow bark tea I've ever had."

Mistress Peevish didn't say, "You're welcome." She just poked her husband in the ribs and said, "Let's go!"

"Yes, my darling," said the mayor, still huffing and puffing, and the two turned to leave.

"Just remember," cried Mistress Peevish on her way out the door, "that goblin's got to go! And fast! The mayor said so! *Didn't you?*" She poked him one more time.

"Yes, cupcake," he replied, and then they were gone.

"Grandmother," Ivy said, "we can't just leave Burdock in the forest, can we?"

"Of course not," answered Grandmother.

"Then we've got to find his parents, don't we?"

"That seems like the only way," said Grandmother.

"Please let me go flying with Cedric and look for them."

"But suppose you find them? The book said you mustn't approach them!"

"I'll only try to find where they live. Then I'll come home, and we can decide what to do next. Would that be all right?"

Grandmother sighed deeply. "If you promise not to go near them. But what will we do with little Burdock while you're away? I'm afraid I'll need somebody to help."

Ivy thought for a minute. "I know!" she said. "I'll ask Peter. He can go and get Edwina and Marta, and the three of them can take care of him. Can you hold him for a minute while I run next door and ask Peter?"

Before long, everything was arranged. Peter and Edwina and Marta could come later in the afternoon, and Cedric was happy to volunteer for a flying job that would take him away from the goblin's noise. While Ivy waited for her friends to arrive, Grandmother sent her to try the new, improved spot-removing potion on Branwen's spots. Branwen was so glad to see Ivy that she whinnied with excitement.

"All right, then," said Ivy, "where would you like me to try it?"

"On my front leg this time," Branwen replied, holding her leg up.

Ivy did as she had seen Grandmother do. She soaked a cloth with potion, then rubbed it all over a small black spot on Branwen's leg, and waited. Ivy and Branwen watched as the spot slowly turned first red . . . then purple . . . then bright blue! "Oh dear," Ivy moaned. "This is not right at all! I'm sorry, Branwen."

Branwen's eyes widened. "Oh," she said. "Blue. How colorful. Now I am a black-and-yellow-and-blue-spotted unicorn." She hung her head down and sighed.

"Maybe Grandmother can try again. She's really very good at making up potions. I'm sure she'll get it right, if she just keeps trying."

"Yes," said Branwen. "Would you ask her to try again, please?"

"Of course I will. But I still think you're very beautiful the way you are! Maybe you just need some more confidence."

"Confidence?" echoed Branwen. "Where will I get that? Surely there's no potion for it."

"I don't know," Ivy said, thinking. "Maybe there could be. I'll try to find out."

Ivy took the jar back to Grandmother and asked her if she would make another spot-removing potion for Branwen when her ankle felt better. "Or maybe," Ivy said, "you could make a potion that would give her more confidence?"

Grandmother said, "Hmm. More confidence. Maybe if Branwen could just believe in herself, she wouldn't need to erase her spots. Unfortunately, there's no potion that can do that."

The Search

Edwina and Marta and Peter just arrived. Ivy invited them in and presented them to Grandmother, telling them about Grandmother's ankle. Ivy explained to them that Cedric would fly her over the Dark Forest to see if they could find any goblins. Then she showed them how to feed mushrooms to Burdock without getting bitten. She showed them how to burp him and how to change his diaper. She warned them that he could climb out of his crate and up the table leg and even up on the cupboard in less than a minute.

"He's kind of cute," said little Marta. "But I wish he wasn't so loud! Can I play with him?"

"Yes," Ivy said, "maybe he'd like that."

Immediately Marta covered her face with her hands and started to play peekaboo with Burdock. When she got to the "BOO!" part, the baby goblin's usual shrieking noise changed to a shriek of laughter. Soon everyone was laughing, even though the noise was as loud as ever.

At last it was time for Ivy to leave. She kissed her grandmother goodbye.

"Remember," Grandmother said, "if you find the goblins, don't approach them. Come home safe to me."

"I will," Ivy promised. She went out the back door and shouted up to Cedric, who was sitting on the roof of the cottage. "Cedric, it's time!" she called.

"*Righto!*" Cedric answered, and he fluttered to the ground, making the air breeze on Ivy's face. He crouched down, so she could climb aboard his broad, feathered back. She arranged herself on his shoulders, with one leg on each side of his neck, and held on tightly.

"I'm ready!" she said, and the griffin made a mighty leap into the air. Ivy gripped his neck, her heart thumping. It was always a thrill to ride on Cedric's back as he cut through the air. Up and up they went, circling over the village and then away toward the Dark Forest.

"Not too high!" Ivy called out as she looked down on the expanse of green. "I can't see anything but treetops." Cedric glided lower over the trees. His hind legs almost touched them as he flew. Ivy looked carefully, but the treetops were clustered so closely together that it was impossible to see the forest floor. She couldn't tell if there were any creatures down there or not.

"Keep going," Ivy cried. "There might be

a clearing where the forest goblins build their houses. Maybe we can find it."

Cedric flapped his mighty wings and swooped to the right. Then to the left. They flew back and forth for miles. On and on they went, Ivy looking below, Cedric looking off in the distance with his eagle eyes. All they saw was a great span of green treetops spreading across the way to the far mountains of the north. The forest spread to Carbuncle Swamp in the east. The village of Broomsweep lay behind them at the edge of the forest in the south. And far off in the west lay another village. They looked until their eyes were tired and stinging, but everything looked the same to them. Finally, Ivy told Cedric to turn back.

"Let's go home by way of the swamp," she said. "Maybe, this time, we can see something at the edge of the forest."

Cedric headed east. Soon they were riding a current of warm, smelly air rising from the swamp. *"Aawk!"* the griffin squawked. "Cedric smells something terrible! Terribly terrible!" The griffin flapped his wings to go higher, away from the smell.

Ivy said, "No! We have to go in lower to look."

Cedric grumbled, but he coasted lower, near the edge of the forest. He focused his eyes on the trees ahead. *"Aawk,"* he said again. "Cedric sees something! Look, look, look!"

"Where?" cried Ivy. Then she saw it. A cluster of big brown lumps that looked like they might be mud huts was sitting on the edge of the swamp, next to the forest. "Go in closer so I can see."

Cedric swooped even lower and skimmed past the mud huts. *Thwack!* went something hard, hitting his beak.

"Aaaawk!!!" went Cedric.

"Ouch!" went Ivy as something hard hit her on the arm. She looked down and saw a hail of stones being thrown at them by creatures that she knew must be goblins. They looked a lot

like Burdock, with their gray skin and bald heads. They were much bigger—about Ivy's size—and not at all cute. They were very ugly, and they were very angry. "Let's get out of here!" Ivy cried.

CHAPTER 12

All Gone

Cedric didn't need to be told twice. He flapped his mighty wings and soared higher, as fast as he could. Ivy could see the edge of the forest and the little town of Broomsweep off in the distance. She gripped Cedric's neck and cried, "Head for home!"

"Home, home, home!" Cedric replied. He flew

straight for Broomsweep as the sunset turned the sky magenta.

Before long, they had landed safely at Grandmother's cottage. Ivy climbed down from Cedric's back and examined his beak to see where the stone had hit him.

"There's a little dent here on your beak," she said, patting him gently. "Does it hurt? Did they hit you anywhere else?"

"Cedric is not hurt," he replied. "Cedric flew out of there fast!"

Ivy examined her arm. "I'm not hurt either—just this tiny bruise. Those goblins were certainly angry!" Ivy could hear Burdock's terrible noise coming from the cottage, and she hurried inside. There, she found Peter and Edwina and Marta all chasing Baby Burdock as he darted around the room, shrieking. He ran and climbed and jumped from the furniture, faster than he had the day before. When he saw Ivy come in, he ran right to her and reached his chubby arms up as if he wanted her to pick him up. Even though he was still squawking, Ivy's heart warmed toward the little creature. He must like her! She picked him up and let him scream in her ear as she spoke loudly to her friends.

"We discovered a village of goblins living next to Carbuncle Swamp!"

Grandmother spoke up from her bed in the corner. "I hope you didn't go too close to them. You remembered what the book said?"

"We couldn't get near them. They threw stones at us. What can we do now, Grandmother?"

"I don't know," said Grandmother. "Maybe the town council will have some ideas. In the meantime, we'll continue taking care of Burdock, just as we have been doing."

Ivy sighed heavily. "If only he wasn't so noisy!"

"And wasn't so energetic!" said Peter.

"And took more naps!" added Marta.

"And didn't cause so much trouble!" cried Edwina.

But Burdock continued to squawk in Ivy's ear, until she put him down. Then he started tearing around the room as he had before.

"I'm tired," complained Peter. "I have to go home."

"We do too," said Edwina.

Ivy thanked them for looking after the baby goblin. Soon she was left to take care of Burdock by herself. All through the evening, Ivy chased him as he bolted about the cottage. She was very hungry, so she took some bread and cheese from the cupboard. She fixed up a plate for Grandmother, then she tried to eat while Burdock bounced on her lap and pulled her hair. At last, she gave up. She fed Burdock some mushrooms and burped him and changed him. She rocked him in her arms until he stopped his noise and went to sleep. By that time, Ivy was so tired she could hardly see straight. She dropped into bed and fell into a deep sleep.

Alas, she did not sleep for long. Twice in the night, she and Grandmother were awakened by the baby's squalling. Twice in the night, Grandmother helped her feed him, and Ivy took care of him and rocked him back to sleep, with her eyes halfway open.

When the sun rose, Ivy tiredly went through the motions again. Feeding, burping, changing, and chasing Burdock. Ivy was so tired, and there was so much to do! Finally she took the squawking baby outside to Cedric's nest. He was covering his ears with his wings. "Cedric," she hollered, "I need you to look after Burdock while I take care of things!"

"Oh no!" moaned Cedric, uncovering his ears. "Griffins don't know how to look after babies!"

"Just keep him in your nest. Grab him if he starts to climb out. *Pleeease*, Cedric?"

He looked unhappy, but he said, "Oh dear, oh

dear. All right. But just for a tiny, little, small while. Cedric's ears are aching already!"

"Thank you, Cedric!" Ivy said as she held out the baby goblin. Cedric reached up with his enormous eagle talons and carefully wrapped them around the tiny baby.

Just then, Farmer Higley arrived, carrying a long, sturdy stick that was forked on one end. "Good morning!" he said. "I heard your grandmother hurt her ankle, so I made her this crutch. Do you think she'd like it?"

"What a good idea!" Ivy said. "Thank you, Farmer Higley. That could be very helpful. You should come inside and give it to Grandmother yourself."

"Oh, that's all right," he replied shyly. "You take it to her. I have to get home and tend my goats. Tell her I'm sorry I gave her that egg. I didn't know it was going to cause so much trouble! That little fellow is certainly loud!"

Ivy only nodded. She said goodbye to Farmer

Higley and thanked him again. She took the crutch inside to Grandmother. Grandmother was very pleased. She carefully put her feet over the side of the bed and used the crutch to stand up. Ivy helped her hobble over to the fireplace to sit on her stool.

"There!" said Grandmother. "Now I can make a new spot-removing potion for Branwen. Would you bring in some wood from the woodpile, and hand me my cooking pot? And please bring me the last spot-removing potion and some chickweed and sassafras."

Ivy did as Grandmother asked, then she left her to her potion-making. She picked up a bag of oats and went to find Branwen in her hiding place under the hazel trees. "Good morning," Ivy said tiredly.

"How can it be a good morning with so much noise?" Branwen replied.

"Well, good morning anyway," said Ivy.

"Does your grandmother have a new spot-removing potion for me?" Branwen asked hope-fully.

"Not yet," Ivy replied. "Her ankle has been hurting her."

"Oh, that's too bad," Branwen said. "I wish I could heal her with my horn, but I just can't. Tell your grandmother I hope she gets well soon."

"Farmer Higley brought her a crutch, so she's doing a little better. She's working on your po-tion now."

Branwen brightened up at this news.

Ivy turned and went about her chores. First she went to find the rabbit with the ear infection, but he was not in his burrow. She called him and called him. He was nowhere to be found. Then she went to find the porcupine who had lost some of her quills. She was nowhere to be found either. Ivy couldn't find the mole with the toothache, and the pixies were still missing. There didn't seem to be any other creatures left in the garden. A big, wet tear rolled down Ivy's cheek.

Ivy returned to the cottage and sadly reported to Grandmother that all the small creatures had gone away.

"Oh dear," Grandmother said, looking very unhappy. "Oh dear, oh dear, oh dear."

CHAPTER 13

Official Business

That morning, while Ivy was looking for the sick creatures, Mistress Peevish and the Honorable Mayor Peevish stood in the town hall with the ten town councilors.

"I tell you, there's a goblin in our midst!" cried Mistress Peevish. "Meg the Healer is keeping it in her cottage! What are you going to do about it?"

"A goblin! Good heavens!" replied one of the councilors.

"Goblins are terrible!" said another.

"Is it a big one?" asked a third.

"Well, no," answered Mistress Peevish. "It's just a small one. But you can't be too careful when it comes to goblins. Who knows, there may be more of them, just waiting to arrive! We've got to put a stop to this before we are all throttled in our beds!"

The mayor stopped chewing his fingernails and looked up at his wife. He pulled on her skirt to get her attention.

"*What?*" she growled.

He started to say something, but no sound came out.

"WHAT IS IT?" she snarled again.

Finally the mayor stuttered, "W-w-well, dearest, how do we *know* they'd th-th-th-throttle us in our beds?"

"They're *goblins*! What more do you need to know?"

"Oh y-y-yes. I suppose you're right," the mayor replied. He went back to chewing on his fingernails.

"Of course I'm right!" Mistress Peevish snapped. "Now, who will come with us to the healer's cottage and tell that woman the goblin has to go?"

The ten town councilors looked at each other and then at Mistress Peevish and the mayor, and each said, "I will!" Then they marched after them out the door of the town hall and down the street all the way to Grandmother's cottage. Before they even got close to the cottage, they could hear the dreadful noise the baby goblin was making.

"There!" said Mistress Peevish. "That's him now!"

"Terrible!" groaned one of the town councilors.

"Horrible!" cried another.

"It mustn't be allowed!" said several others.

"Maybe he's unhappy," said the mayor softly, but no one paid any attention.

When the group arrived at Grandmother's cottage, Mistress Peevish marched right up to the door and knocked loudly.

Ivy answered the door. "Grandmother, we have company!" she called when she saw that it was the mayor and his wife and the whole town council.

"Oh, do invite them in," replied Grandmother. She had to shout to make herself heard over Burdock's racket. So in they came. First Mistress Peevish, then the mayor, then each of the ten town councilors. Burdock looked at the crowd of people and bellowed even louder.

"Terrible!"

"Horrible!"

"It mustn't be allowed!" said the town councilors.

Quickly, Ivy picked up a basket of mushrooms

and began to feed them to Burdock. He couldn't eat and holler at the same time, so it suddenly became quiet—except for his slurping.

"So nice of you to come by!" said Grandmother.

"Never mind that!" replied Mistress Peevish. "We're here on official business—about the goblin."

"Oh yes. The noise. It's quite a problem," Grandmother said.

"Well, you can't have a *goblin* here anyway!" Mistress Peevish objected. "That's been settled. No goblins in Broomsweep! Isn't that so?" she said to the mayor as she poked him in the ribs.

"If you say so, my lovely," the mayor replied.

"I do!" his wife cried.

"But . . . ," spluttered Ivy. "But we put up a sign saying *Magical Creatures Welcome!*"

"Well, we've decided that doesn't apply to goblins! Maybe we'd better take the sign down!"

"But where will he go?" Ivy interrupted. "We

can't just leave him in the forest! He's too little to take care of himself."

"That's not our concern!" responded Mistress Peevish. The town councilors all agreed.

"What we need is a way to return him to his own people," said Grandmother. "Who among you is brave enough to go talk to the goblins?"

CHAPTER 14

A Plan

The town councilors turned pale. Two of them had to sit down quickly. "It's certainly not *our* job to talk to goblins!" said a third. "The *idea*!"

"We don't know where to find them anyway," said a fourth.

"*I* found them," said Ivy. "They have a village next to Carbuncle Swamp. Cedric took me flying, and we found them. But we couldn't talk to them. They threw stones at us."

"Of *course* they did!" said another councilor. "I've heard they're terrible creatures! Moody and violent!"

"And also quite ugly!" added another. "So I've heard tell."

"We can't talk to such creatures!" exclaimed the mayor's wife. "It's out of the question!"

"Perhaps you could find someone who would," said Grandmother.

"It's your goblin, so it's *your job,*" Mistress Peevish announced.

"Yes!" pronounced one of the councilors.

"Quite right!" exclaimed another.

"Entirely yours," the town councilors agreed, and they hurried to leave.

"We're coming back in two days," cried Mistress Peevish. "That little goblin had better be gone by then! Isn't that right?" she said to the mayor, poking him in the ribs.

"I suppose you're right, bunny," he replied.

"*Of course* I'm right!" she added, and with that, she and the mayor and all ten of the town councilors left Ivy and Grandmother to solve the problem by themselves.

Burdock finished eating and began to make his terrible noise again. Grandmother looked sad and tired. Ivy tried to think, but the clamor made it hard. Burdock had driven away the pixies and all the little animals who needed Grandmother's help. His noise was getting on Cedric's nerves, keeping Balthazar from his sleep, and making the neighbors angry. And he was making terrible trouble for her grandmother. Something had to be done. But what?

Ivy thought the only answer was to find Burdock's goblin parents to take care of him. But how? What if she took Burdock to the goblin village? The goblins seemed so mean. What if they were mean to little Burdock too? Ivy couldn't stand to think about that. Someone had to go see what the goblins were really like and talk to them. Grandmother couldn't go because of her injured ankle. Mistress Peevish wouldn't go. The mayor wouldn't go. None of the town councilors would go. Maybe Ivy would have to go herself.

Ivy started to form a plan. She was afraid of the Dark Forest, and she was afraid of the goblins. Should she take someone with her for protection? What about Cedric? But the goblins had already thrown stones at Cedric. Maybe if she went by herself, a little girl all alone, they would know she came in peace.

If only they were peaceful, if only they would listen! Then Burdock could be restored to his parents. The terrible noise would be gone. The sick animals could come back to Grandmother's garden to be healed. And maybe, just maybe, the pixies would return. They could all live happily ever after again!

For the rest of that day, while she took care of

Burdock, she made her plans. It was a long way to Carbuncle Swamp. It might take her most of a day to get there on foot. She could follow the path to Carbuncle Swamp, then travel along the edge of the forest until she came to the goblins' village. She would need to take food and water.

And someone would have to take care of Burdock while she was gone. This seemed to be the biggest problem of all. Who could take care of the baby goblin all day, and even in the night? Someone who had no other job to do. Someone who knew how to take care of a baby. Suddenly Ivy thought of Mistress Peevish. Mistress Peevish had showed her the right way to put on Burdock's diaper. And Mistress Peevish had helped Grandmother by making willow bark tea. Maybe she would help her again.

Early the next morning, before Burdock and Grandmother awoke, Ivy packed a basket with some supplies. Then she stowed the basket by the back steps, and ran to the mayor's house.

She knocked loudly on the door, but no one answered. "Mistress Peevish!" she called out. "Mistress Peevish, it's me, Ivy!" She kept knocking until finally the door opened a crack.

A very cranky voice called out, "What is it? Go away! It's too early for visitors!"

"Mistress Peevish, please help! I have to go into the Dark Forest and gather more mushrooms. It's the only way to keep the baby quiet! Grandmother will need your help taking care of Burdock. Please come quickly before Burdock wakes up!"

"Me? Help you take care of that goblin? Is this a joke?"

"Please, Mistress Peevish. It's no joke. Grandmother still can't walk without a crutch. She'll never be able to keep up with a baby goblin. Not like you can. Her ankle is still hurting her. And she needs more willow bark tea. And nobody can make it quite the way you do!"

There was silence from within the house.

"Please, Mistress Peevish! Won't you please come?"

There was more silence. And more silence. Then the door opened, and Mistress Peevish looked at Ivy's hopeful face. "Oh, very well," she said. "I'll come as soon as I'm dressed. But *don't think* that this is going to change my mind!"

"Oh, thank you, Mistress Peevish!" Ivy cried. And she ran home again. She still didn't hear any noise coming from the cottage. In just a few minutes, Mistress Peevish came down the street. Ivy met her at the door and whispered, "I'm going to go talk to the goblins. Please tell my grandmother not to worry about me. I'll be back as soon as I can." Ivy felt terrible, because she knew Grandmother *would* worry about her, but it seemed like the only way.

"But you're only a little girl!" cried Mistress Peevish. "It's too dangerous!"

"No one else will go—so it's up to me!" replied Ivy. With that, Ivy darted around the cottage to the back door and got her basket. She looked toward the Dark Forest and gulped.

CHAPTER 15

SILENCE!

Ivy walked quickly down the road to the forest. All too soon she understood how the Dark
Forest got its name; it really was dark! The treetops blocked out the sun and made everything
look green. All around her were trees and trees
and more trees. They all looked the same. Ivy
knew that if she stepped off the road, she would
be lost. The woods were full of shadows. She

watched the shadows for hidden goblins, even though she was not near their village yet. She listened for scary sounds, but all she heard were birdcalls.

On and on Ivy walked. After a while, she got tired and hungry. She sat down by the side of the road and took some bread and cheese from her basket. A squirrel came up to her and looked hungry too, so she shared some of her food with it. Having some company made her feel better for a little while. The squirrel took some pieces of cheese from her hand and then skittered away up a tree. Ivy was alone again.

"Well," she said to herself, "I might as well keep going." She got up and went on her way. The sun was high in the sky now, but the forest stayed cool. Ivy breathed in the fresh air and listened to the birdcalls. She began to think the forest was not quite such a scary place after all, but she still watched the shadows for hidden goblins.

After a long while, the air seemed to change. It

was not so fresh anymore. It began to smell like rotten eggs—and cow farts! Ivy knew she was getting closer to Carbuncle Swamp. The road was getting narrower as she went along. Pretty soon it was only a path. What if she lost her way? Then she might never find the goblins. And how would she ever find her way home? The path became harder to make out. Finally, she could see no path at all. Which way was the swamp?

The trees seemed to crowd in on her. Ivy tried to be brave. She whistled to cheer herself up. She thought of Grandmother. Was Grandmother thinking of her? Worrying about her? Maybe she should not have come into the Dark Forest all by herself. Little prickles of fear went up Ivy's spine.

The shadows seemed darker now. Ivy walked around and around, looking for some sign of the path. Suddenly she tripped over a low branch. Something swooped up around her. It was a trap! She was caught in a big net, hanging from a tree. Ivy tried to wriggle free, but she couldn't. She started to panic.

"Help!" she cried. *"Help! Help! Help!"*

Out of the shadows came some dark figures. They were about as big as Ivy, but they walked hunched over. They were gray-skinned and bald, like Burdock. They had big, warty noses, long white fangs, and pointed ears. Goblins!

"Look! We've caught a human!" said one.

"She's trespassing!" said another. "This is *our* land!"

"Humans are egg stealers!" said a third.

"Egg stealer! Egg stealer!" they all began to cry.

Ivy tried to say, "No, I'm not!" but the goblins' noise drowned her out.

"TAKE HER TO THE CHIEF!" shouted one goblin. "LET HIM DECIDE WHAT TO DO WITH HER!"

Another goblin shouted, "YES! TAKE HER TO THE CHIEF! HE'LL KNOW WHAT TO DO WITH HER!"

The other goblins shouted, "YES! YES! TAKE HER TO THE CHIEF! MAYBE HE'LL LET US ROAST HER FOR SUPPER!"

Some of the goblins cut down the net. "Oh! She's so *ugly*!" they all agreed. Then two of them grabbed Ivy by the arms and dragged her away. Two of the others fought over her basket.

Ivy tried again to say, "I'm not an egg stealer!" but one of the goblins shook her arm and cried, "SILENCE, HUMAN!"

Ivy decided to keep silent until she could talk to the chief.

It seemed like they dragged her a very long way. The goblins whooped and hollered. They were overjoyed to have Ivy as a prisoner. Ivy trembled. She didn't want to get in trouble with the chief! She didn't want to be roasted for supper! Would the chief listen to her? She could tell they were getting closer to the swamp, because the terrible swamp smell was getting stronger. Ivy tried to hold her breath, but she couldn't do it for very long. At last she saw some mud huts in the distance. It was the goblin village. Soon a horde of goblins came from the village and joined them. Big ones and little ones. They all whooped and hollered some more. Ivy shivered. *It was a big mistake to come here,* she thought. Would she ever see Grandmother again?

Finally they came to the doorway of a mud hut that looked even muddier than all the rest. Big goblins stood on either side of the door, guarding it. One of the goblins holding Ivy said, "We have brought an egg stealer to the chief!"

One of the guards went in the hut. When he came back out again, he said, "Chief Earwig is coming! Hail to the chief!"

All the hollering goblins suddenly stopped their hollering and said, "Hail to Chief Earwig!" Then they were mostly quiet.

Out of the doorway stepped a little old goblin. His eyes were cloudy. His gray skin was faded and wrinkled. He wore a long cape and held a scepter made of a big, crooked stick.

"Bring forth the egg stealer," he croaked.

The goblins who were holding Ivy pushed her up to stand in front of the chief.

"You are on our land, egg stealer!" said Chief Earwig loudly.

"I'm not an egg stea—" Ivy tried to say once

again, but one of the guards looked her in the face and roared, "SILENCE!"

"One of our eggs was stolen from its hiding place!" announced Chief Earwig. "We could smell human all around there. A human took our egg! In return, we will keep you here with us! You will work for us forever!"

CHAPTER 16

Too Much Mud

Ivy's heart seemed to thump extra hard. "But the egg—" she opened her mouth to say.

"SILENCE! EGG STEALERS MUST NOT SPEAK!" shouted a guard.

"But—" Ivy tried once more, and the chief said, "One more word out of you, and you'll be sorry!"

Ivy was getting a headache. At least the chief hadn't said she should be roasted for supper.

She decided to wait and find some other way to talk to him.

"Put her to work!" said Chief Earwig. Two goblins grabbed her and dragged her away. They took her to a place where several goblins were trying to build a mud hut. One of them was pounding sticks into the ground to make a wall. Another mixed up a vat of smelly mud with small pebbles. A third slopped the mixture on the sticks and filled in between them.

"What's the worst part of your job?" one of the goblin guards asked.

"The worst part is hauling mud from the swamp!" answered another one of the goblins.

"Then make *her* do it!" said the guard, and he pushed Ivy toward the goblins.

"Oho! This will be good!" a goblin said.

Another shoved two wooden buckets at her, one for each hand. "Come with me!" he commanded, heading for the swamp.

Ivy had no choice but to pick up the buckets

and follow. The goblin led her to the edge of the slimy brown swamp water and waded in.

"Here's what you do," he growled. "You reach down and pull up handfuls of mud from the bottom and throw them into the buckets, like this." Then he showed her how it was done. He reached down under the swamp water and pulled up sloppy handfuls of wet mud. He threw them into a bucket on the shore.

"When the buckets are full, you carry them back to us. And don't bother trying to run away. There will always be someone watching you, no matter where you go! Get to work, or you'll have no supper!"

Ivy wondered what they might give her to eat. She was pretty sure she wouldn't like it, but she didn't want to starve. Sighing, she took off her shoes and waded into the brown water. Hiking up her skirt, she bent over to dig up handfuls of the slimy mud. She could feel it squishing between her fingers, and it made her feel sick. It also made her back ache to bend over so much. But she kept going and threw more handfuls of mud into the buckets. The smell made Ivy want to hold her breath, but she kept going and threw *more* handfuls of mud into the buckets.

As she worked, Ivy snuck peeks at the goblins around her. Some wore short garments, and some wore longer ones. She figured out that the ones wearing longer garments were probably women goblins. Some goblins were looking after young ones and babies like Burdock. She tried to keep an eye on them to see how they treated their children. The youngsters ran around, getting into things, just like Burdock. Some were splashing in the brown swamp water. Some were running in and out of the mud huts or between the grown-ups' legs. Some were climbing trees and jumping out of them. But the grown-up goblins didn't seem to mind. They just sang a song to them. She noticed that none of the babies here screeched like Burdock. *Why not?* she wondered.

Had she and Grandmother been doing something wrong?

By this time, Ivy was soaking wet and covered in mud. She worked on. Little by little, the buckets filled up until finally they were full. Ivy rested for a minute, then she tried to lift one of the buckets. It was so heavy she couldn't do it. Not with one hand. Not with both hands. She didn't know what to do. How could she call for help if she was not allowed to speak?

Finally one of the women goblins, who had been sitting off by herself, got up and came over to her. "You're too feeble to lift that!" she said. The goblin easily lifted one bucket in each hand and grunted for Ivy to follow her.

When they reached the place where the goblins were making the mud hut, the woman who had helped Ivy set down the buckets and called the others by name. "Pigwort! Walnut! Beetle! What do you mean by giving this child such a hard job? She can't lift these buckets by herself!"

The one called Beetle spoke up. "The guard said to give her the hardest job, so we did!"

"Since when do we punish human children?"

"Ask the chief!"

"I will!"

The woman goblin took Ivy by the arm and marched right up to the chief's mud hut. "Tell the chief Mulberry wants to talk to him," she told the guards.

One of them went into the mud hut. After a

minute, he poked his head out of the door and said, "You may come in."

Mulberry pulled Ivy into the hut with her and faced the chief.

"Chief Earwig," she began, "why are you punishing this child?"

The chief looked calmly at Mulberry and said, "She is an egg stealer! We have taken her in return for the egg that was stolen. It is only fair and just."

"Then I claim her for myself. It was my egg that was stolen, after all."

CHAPTER 17

War Party

Ivy gasped. She forgot about staying silent and said, "You? You're Burdock's mother?"

Mulberry's mouth fell open. She grabbed Ivy by both shoulders and stared her in the face. "What did you say? Whose mother? Quickly, child, what do you know of my egg?"

Ivy looked at the chief. "May I speak?"

"SPEAK!" said the chief.

Ivy hardly knew where to start, so she started at the beginning. "Farmer Higley found an egg. He didn't know it was a goblin's egg. He brought it to my grandmother. She is a healer of all kinds of creatures, but we didn't know at first what it was either. But then the egg hatched! And it was a baby goblin. And we named him Burdock. We had to look in a book to see how to feed him, and—"

Mulberry shook Ivy's shoulders and cried, "You have him? You have my baby?"

"Yes! My grandmother does! That's why I came here, to see about giving him back to you."

"Ahh, WONDERFUL!" Mulberry said, hugging Ivy close. "And—Burdock! What a wonderful name! It's just what I would have chosen myself!"

"WAIT!" commanded the chief. "Don't be so eager to believe what this human says! Humans cannot be trusted. It could be a trick. She would probably say anything to escape captivity!"

"No!" cried Ivy. "I give you my word!"

"Your word carries no weight with me, human."

Mulberry's face fell. She backed away from Ivy and looked directly into her eyes. Ivy looked directly back. "I believe her," Mulberry said, after a minute.

"Of course you want to believe her," said the chief. "Your thoughts are clouded by your feelings."

"Please, Chief," Ivy began, "if you would only take me back to my village—"

"SILENCE! You have said enough."

Ivy closed her mouth again.

"If we go to the human village, we may be attacked. Therefore, I shall take a war party," pronounced the chief. "If they return our cub to us, we set the child free. If not, we keep her forever!"

Ivy was filled with relief. Grandmother would willingly exchange Burdock for Ivy, and all would be well again!

"We leave at dawn," Chief Earwig said.

He sent Ivy to stay with Mulberry and her

mate, Thistle, in their small mud hut. When it came time for supper, Mulberry taught Ivy how to make mushroom stew. Ivy thought that it was actually quite good, but she wouldn't want to eat it every day. That night, she lay on the dirt floor to sleep as Mulberry and Thistle did. She missed her own bed. She missed Cedric and Balthazar and the pixies. Most of all, she missed Grandmother. A tear ran down her cheek as she thought of home. Finally, she slept.

Back at Grandmother's cottage, Mistress Peevish was having a hard time getting Burdock to settle down for bed. One minute, he was climbing up on the furniture and jumping off again. The next minute, he was running around the cottage, banging a big spoon on everything in sight. He even banged the spoon on Mistress Peevish's head. It made a *thunk*ing sound. And all the time, he was shrieking so loudly that Mistress Peevish thought her ears would break. Mistress Peevish was miserable. She had felt terrible when Ivy ran off into the Dark Forest. And she had felt even worse when she'd had to explain to Grandmother that Ivy had gone to face the goblins alone.

"Oh, where is my little Ivy?" Grandmother had moaned.

Now, as night was falling, Grandmother asked again, "Where is my little Ivy? What if the goblins have her? Will they be kind to her? Will she ever come home again?" A tear ran down her cheek as she stared out the window.

The next morning, the goblins and Ivy were up with the sun. Chief Earwig gathered his war party. Ivy saw Pigwort, Walnut, and Beetle and several of the guards. There were twenty goblins in the war party, including Mulberry and Thistle and the chief. They were all ready with packs of food and sharp spears and shields. Ivy hoped there wouldn't be any trouble. They set off to find the road to Broomsweep, with Chief Earwig in the lead. He was very slow. For a long time, they traveled along the edge of the swamp. After a while, they came to the path that Ivy had followed. And after another long while, the path widened into a road.

Chief Earwig kept Ivy by his side. She was supposed to take them to Grandmother's cottage to find Burdock. They marched all through the morning and through the afternoon without stopping, even to eat. Ivy got very hungry and tired, but she didn't dare complain. When they finally reached the edge of the Dark Forest, Ivy asked the chief to leave the war party there. She didn't want to upset Cedric or Balthazar or Grandmother or Mistress Peevish or Branwen or any of the villagers.

Cedric watched from his perch on top of the cottage while Ivy and Mulberry and Thistle and

Chief Earwig walked out of the Dark Forest and came toward the house.

"*Aawk!* Goblins!" he squawked. The feathers on his head stood straight up.

"It's all right, Cedric!" Ivy cried. "They come in peace!"

Cedric settled back down, but he kept his eagle eyes on the goblins.

Inside Grandmother's cottage, Mistress Peevish was feeding Burdock his supper of mushrooms. He couldn't eat and shriek at the same time, so he wasn't yelping at all. She held him on her lap with one arm while she fed him with her other hand. Mistress Peevish forgot to be grumpy about taking care of him. She even thought that he was rather cute, with his button nose and little, blunt fangs. He felt warm on her lap, and she cuddled him close. When he was done eating his mushrooms, she even gave him some apple slices for dessert.

Right away she could tell that something was

wrong! Burdock began to look sick. He felt much too warm, and he began to cough. First his mouth turned green, then his cheeks, then his whole face turned green. Soon his arms and legs and hands and feet turned green too.

Just then, Ivy walked in the front door. Behind her were Chief Earwig, Mulberry, and Thistle. Mulberry took one look at little green Burdock and said, "Oh no! What have you done?"

Mistress Peevish was shocked to see the goblins there, but she answered, "I gave him some apple slices for dessert!"

"You've given him apples! Oh no! You must never give apples to baby goblins! My poor baby! What will become of him?" Mulberry picked him up and held him tightly as he coughed. "He's much too warm!"

Thistle put his arm around Mulberry's shoulder and choked back a sob. "Green!" he said. "Our son is *green*!"

CHAPTER 18

Ivy's Idea

Grandmother put her hand on Burdock's head. "What can we do for him?" she asked.

"Nothing. There's nothing you can do," said Mulberry.

"I didn't know!" Mistress Peevish said. "I'm so sorry!"

Everyone felt bad. Even the chief. But he was angry too. He stepped back outside and signaled the war party to come. Cedric was still on the roof of the cottage, keeping watch over the garden. When he saw all the goblins coming, he squawked a mighty squawk. *"Aawk!* Goblins! Gob-gob-goblins! *Aawk!"* He spread his enormous wings and opened his beak. He hissed at the goblins and looked terrifying.

When the war party reached the cottage, the chief told them that the baby goblin had been fed apples. Soon the cottage was surrounded by angry goblins.

Mistress Peevish said, "I knew it! The goblins have come to take over the town!"

"Hush," Grandmother told her.

Ivy heard Cedric squawking. Before anyone could stop her, she ran out of the cottage and hollered up to him, "Calm down, Cedric! We don't want any trouble!"

Cedric slowly closed his wings, but he kept on hissing. Then Ivy saw Balthazar coming up the path from the stream. The old dragon blew some flaming breath, as if he was ready to do battle. "Let be at theb! Let be at theb!" he cried.

She called out to him, "Calm down, Balthazar! We don't want any trouble!"

Then she saw Branwen come out from under the hazel trees. She looked ready to do some damage with her horn.

Ivy called out to her, "Calm down, Branwen! We don't want—" Then suddenly Ivy got an idea. "Wait!" she cried. "There's one thing we can try."

She said to Mulberry, "Bring him out into the garden! Hurry!"

Mulberry carried the baby goblin outside while Ivy called Branwen to come to her. For a minute, it looked as if the war party wouldn't let Branwen pass, but the chief gave a signal and they finally parted and let her through.

"Branwen," Ivy cried, "the baby goblin ate something he shouldn't have, and now he's very sick! You've got to heal him with your horn!"

Branwen's eyes widened. "But I can't! I'm not

a real unicorn. My horn doesn't work! I've tried it before, and nothing happens!"

"You can heal him!" Ivy insisted. "You just need to have some confidence. I believe in you, Branwen. We *all* believe in you! Don't we?" she cried.

Grandmother came hobbling through the door. "I believe in you!" she said. "You can do it, Branwen. Just touch him with your horn, and think good thoughts. Think hard!"

Even Mistress Peevish came to the door and cried, "You can do it! Surely you can do it!"

Soon Mulberry and Thistle took up the cry, and then the chief joined in. He ordered all the goblins to put down their weapons, and they began to chant too. "You can do it!"

Cedric and Balthazar saw the baby goblin in Mulberry's arms and heard what was happening. They felt terrible that the noisy little goblin was sick. "You can do it!" they cried to Branwen.

Branwen's eyes filled with tears. Did everyone *really* believe in *her*? Was it possible? Could she be a real unicorn after all? Could she heal the sick baby? She looked at Baby Burdock in his mother's arms and knew she had to try. She bent her head down and softly touched the baby's heart with the tip of her horn. She thought of being a real unicorn. That made her so happy that she felt a deep warmth come from her own heart and rise up and out through her horn. She held her horn against Burdock's chest for a minute while everyone chanted "You can do it" and "I believe in you." She started to believe she *could* do it.

Burdock stopped coughing! The green began to fade away. Burdock's hands and feet were no longer green. Then his face and mouth were no longer green.

"He's cooling off!" announced Mulberry.

And then Burdock began to screech. Everyone cheered! Branwen was so happy she almost glowed.

Burdock looked up at Mulberry and Thistle, and he suddenly screeched louder. Then he leaped into Ivy's arms and clung to her. He didn't know his own parents. He wanted Ivy. Everyone was delighted that little Burdock was all better, but now no one knew what to do. What if the baby goblin wanted to stay with Ivy?

Finally, the chief said, "This baby has been raised by humans. Now he thinks that he is a human too. But can the humans stop his screeching?"

Mulberry smiled. "I can," she said. She began to sing softly. Ivy remembered that song. It was the song that the goblins had been singing to their young ones back in the goblin village. None of the little goblins in the village had been screeching.

Now Burdock seemed to listen to Mulberry's soft song. Thistle joined in the singing.

Little goblin, soft and sweet,
smells of swamp and dirty feet,
plays in mud and climbs in trees,
picks its nose and scratches fleas.
Little goblin, sweet and clever,
stop your screeching now forever!

Burdock suddenly stopped screeching. He held his arms out to Mulberry and went to her. "Ahh," sighed everyone.

CHAPTER 19

A Picnic

Chief Earwig smiled. Then everyone smiled. Even Mistress Peevish smiled. Only Ivy and Grandmother felt a little sad that Burdock would be leaving them.

"Can he come back for visits?" Ivy asked the chief.

The chief thought hard for a minute. Then

he called Burdock's parents over to him. They whispered back and forth for another minute.

Finally, Chief Earwig spoke. "This baby goblin shall live with his parents, but these humans gave him his first home. Therefore, he shall come back and visit once every moon. He shall be a link between goblins and humans. And when he is grown, he shall be the keeper of the peace between us. I have spoken."

Ivy liked that plan. So did Grandmother. They smiled happily. "Won't you stay and celebrate with us?" said Grandmother. "We could have a picnic in the garden."

The goblins thought that was a great idea. All twenty of them sat down and unpacked their food. The chief sat with Ivy and Grandmother. They had a nice talk. Branwen and Cedric and Balthazar joined them. Everyone made a big fuss over Branwen. She was the hero of the day. Ivy made a daisy chain and draped it around the unicorn's neck.

Little Burdock ran back and forth between his parents and Ivy and Grandmother. Sometimes Mulberry or Thistle would sing to him, and he didn't screech at all. Mulberry taught Ivy the song too.

At first, Mistress Peevish didn't want to sit down and picnic with the goblins. "Look at all these goblins," she said. "I told you that more goblins would come and take over the town! They might still throttle us in our sleep."

But Grandmother said, "They aren't going to throttle you in your sleep. They just wanted their baby back. Now sit down and hush!"

And Mistress Peevish did.

After a while, the mayor came looking for her. "What's this?" he cried. "A picnic? With goblins? What's going on?"

"Sit down and hush!" said Mistress Peevish. And he did.

Pretty soon Peter and his parents came to see what was going on. "It's a goblin invasion!" said Jacob the Baker.

"But look!" cried Peter. "Everyone is smiling and laughing!"

"So they are! And the little goblin has stopped screeching!" said Jacob the Baker. "Hurray!" He went and fetched three trays of muffins from his shop and brought them to share.

Then the ten town councilors showed up. They came to make sure

that the baby goblin was leaving. But when they got there, instead of one baby goblin, there was a whole gathering of goblins. They saw their spears and shields lying on the ground.

"It's a war party!" said one.

"This is terrible!" said another.

"Horrible!" said a third.

"It mustn't be allowed!" said the rest.

But the mayor said, "Listen! There's no more screeching! The baby goblin's people have come to find him. Look at all the happy faces. This is not a war party. It's just a party! Isn't it, cupcake?" he said, turning to his wife.

Mistress Peevish smiled at them. "Why don't you sit down and join us?" she said.

And so they did.

They watched as Burdock taught himself to do somersaults in the garden. Just as the fun was getting started, Mistress Peevish's golden-furred dog, Foof, peeked out of the bushes. Mistress Peevish was delighted. She called to her. Foof slowly crept out of the bushes. Then she barked three times, and three little puppies followed along behind her. Poof came up behind them and barked happily. Burdock and the puppies were running and rolling and doing somersaults. Before long, the goblins and the humans were laughing together over their antics.

And that is the story of how the humans of Broomsweep got to be friends with the forest goblins, and how Branwen found her confidence. After the goblins took Burdock home, things settled down at Grandmother's cottage. Grandmother told Ivy that she must never again go off into the Dark Forest alone, and Ivy promised that she wouldn't. She was not allowed to go outside of the garden again for a long time.

Grandmother's ankle got all better, and before long, she didn't need her crutch anymore.

Branwen never again asked Grandmother to erase her spots. "I am a real, one-of-a-kind, black-and-yellow-and-blue-spotted unicorn," she said, holding her head up high. And Ivy and Grandmother agreed.

Mistress Peevish said she couldn't break up a family, so Foof and her puppies stayed on in the garden. No one ever found their hiding place.

After all the racket stopped, Balthazar got some sleep and his cold got better. Cedric greeted Ivy every day with a "Good, good, good morning!" After a while, the rabbit with the earache came scratching at Grandmother's back door again. Later, the porcupine came back. Then the mole with the toothache came back too and brought along a groundhog with a wounded paw and a turtle with a chipped shell. Grandmother and Ivy took care of them all, and that made Ivy happy.

Still, Ivy missed Burdock. She missed his warm, little body and his big, round eyes. She missed the excitement when he would run all around in the cottage, jumping on things. She missed how sweet he looked when he finally went to sleep.

But every month, Mulberry and Thistle brought Burdock back to Broomsweep for a visit. Everyone was glad to see him. Sometimes, Mistress Peevish would come too. Since she had taken care of Baby Burdock, her nice side had grown several sizes. They all took turns singing the goblins' song, and there was no more screeching. As Burdock grew, so did the friendship between the goblins and the humans.

But still, something was missing.

Every day, after Ivy had taken care of all the creatures in the garden, she put a fresh cup of honey in the hole in the oak tree. She hoped and hoped that the pixies would come back.

And then, one day, they did!

Ivy was scattering some seeds for the birds, and suddenly a tiny girl pixie landed on her right shoulder. Ivy stood very still, and said softly, "Hello, little pixie. I'm so delighted to see you! I'm sorry if the noise scared you away. We missed you!" Then the air started buzzing with pixies. Soon they were alighting on her head and arms and shoulders. It was their special greeting. The pixies were back!

And Ivy was living happily ever after once again.